This book belongs to:

_____

_____

_____

First published by Walker Books Ltd.
87 Vauxhall Walk, London SE11 5HJ

Based on the audio visual series "Maisy." A King Rollo Films production for
Universal Pictures International Visual Programming. Original script by Andrew Brenner.
Illustrated in the style of Lucy Cousins by King Rollo Films Ltd.

First U.S. edition 2002

Library of Congress Cataloging-in-Publication Data

Cousins, Lucy.
Maisy makes lemonade / Lucy Cousins. —1st U.S. ed.
p.   cm.
Summary: On a hot day, Maisy the mouse and
Eddie the elephant make lemonade and enjoy it together.
ISBN 0-7636-1728-8 (hardcover)—ISBN 0-7636-1729-6 (paperback)
[1. Mice—Fiction. 2. Elephants—Fiction. 3. Lemonade—Fiction.] I. Title.
PZ7.C83175 Maig 2002
[E]—dc21   2001035634

2 4 6 8 10 9 7 5 3

Printed in Hong Kong

This book was typeset in Lucy Cousins.
The illustrations were done in gouache.

Candlewick Press
2067 Massachusetts Avenue
Cambridge, Massachusetts 02140

visit us at www.candlewick.com

Maisy Makes Lemonade

Lucy Cousins

CANDLEWICK PRESS
CAMBRIDGE, MASSACHUSETTS

It's hot today.
Maisy is having a
nice cold drink.

Mmmm. Lemonade.

Eddie is hot, too. Maisy shares the lemonade.

Eddie takes a big drink . . .

...and it's all gone!

Poor Eddie.
He is very thirsty.

Maisy has an idea.

She goes to
the lemon tree in
the garden.

She picks some fruit — with a little help from Eddie!

In the kitchen,
Eddie squeezes lemon
juice into a pitcher.

Maisy adds
water.

Then Eddie stirs in some sugar.

There! A fresh pitcher of delicious lemonade.

Maisy goes to get the cups.

Slurp!

What's that noise?

It's Eddie!
He couldn't wait.

But there's plenty for
Maisy, too. Good job!

Lucy Cousins is one of today's most acclaimed author-illustrators of children's books. Her unique titles instantly engage babies, toddlers, and preschoolers with their childlike simplicity and bright colors. And the winsome exploits of characters like Maisy reflect the adventures that young children have every day.

Lucy admits that illustration comes more easily to her than writing, which tends to work around the drawings. "I draw by heart," she says. "I think of what children would like by going back to my own childlike instincts." And what instincts! Lucy Cousins now has more than three million books in print, from cloth and picture books to irresistible pull-the-tab and lift-the-flap books.